MORALS

So far in the Series

Fartin' Martin Sidebottom is a boy who can't stop breaking wind - and joins a brass band conducted by The Devil.

Black-Toothed Ruth Black never brushes her teeth - and gets carried away by the evil tooth devils.

Fidgety Bridget Wrigglesworth has ants in her pants and can't keep still in class - So The Anthill Mob come calling.

Nose-picking Nicholas Pickering can't stop picking his nose - and ends up having a terrifying confrontation with The Bogeyman.

Messy Bessie Clutterbuck won't keep her bedroom tidy - and finds herself in the biggest mess of her life at Devil's Dump.

Daydreaming Daisy McCloud Can't concentrate in class - So dark clouds gather.

Coming Soon

Hairy Harriet Harrison is a warning to anyone who doesn't brush their hair - poor Harriet gets lost in a frightening jungle.

Gobby Nobby Robinson can't stop talking - and is caught in a deadly mouth-trap.

Smelly Simon Smedley won't change his socks - So Bigfoot pays a visit.

Grubby Joe Grub refuses to get washed - So he turns into a dirty pig. Can anyone save his bacon?

Scruffy Davy Duffy won't dress smartly - So werewolf scarecrows make him change his ways.

Kipping Kevin Kipling won't get out of bed - So the bed bugs and The Sandman sound the alarm.

ISBN - 978-1-908211-54-5

First Published in Great Britain in 2016 by Pro-actif Communications
Cameron House, 42 Swinburne Road, Darlington, Co Durham DL3 7TD
Email: books@carpetbombingculture.co.uk
Pro-actif Communications

Peter Barron
The right of Peter Barron to be identified as the author of this work has been asserted by him in accordance with the Copyright, Design and Patents act of 1988.

www.monstrousmorals.co.uk

Chilly Billy Winters

Children be warned - wrap up warm when there's ice,
for the horrors that follow are not very nice...

There was never a boy like my little friend Billy,
For being so silly when the weather turned chilly.
Billy Winters was told to wrap up nice and warm,
"Flu can be deadly," his mother would warn.

Her pleas grew more desperate as the air became colder,
But Billy ignored her - she just got the cold shoulder.
"Wear your hat," cried his Mum, "some gloves and a vest,"
But you'd think it was summer, the way Billy was dressed.

Wearing gloves and a hat made him feel like a fool,
And vests were for wimps, not for boys who were cool.
A t-shirt would do - being cold didn't matter,
Who cared if the winter winds made his teeth chatter?

His jumpers were baggy, not one of them fitted,
And as for the scarf his mother had knitted,
It was soft, green and red but, sadly, it stayed,
Round the neck of the snowman Billy had made.

Gentle and kind, he'd been built near the shed,
The snowman was given a name - Frozen Fred.
Fred was distinguished - he had class, he had charm,
He carried a broomstick under one arm.

With a hat to go with his scarf, he had style,
A twig from an oak tree gave him a smile.
For eyes, lumps of coal were fitted in place,
While a large, wonky carrot completed his face.

One day in December, with temperatures dropping,
Billy's Mum went out for her grocery shopping.
Left all by himself, Billy was napping,
But awoke to the sound of a curious tapping.

As he looked on in horror, more faces stared back,
The air was so frosty, the window went CRACK!
Twelve snowmen, each wearing a wicked expression,
Had come to teach Billy a cold-hearted lesson.

They pushed at the window and clambered inside,
Billy was helpless, there was nowhere to hide.
They grabbed at his t-shirt, he shivered with fright,
As they flew through the window, out into the night.

These weren't nice, friendly snowmen like old Frozen Fred,
They were evil snow zombies, come back from the dead.
As they flew through the clouds, a flock of snow geese,
Kept pecking at Billy, so the boy got no peace.

He was carried through hailstones, bigger than rocks,
Billy was sorry he'd not worn thicker socks.
His fingers and toes were so cold they went numb,
He was starting to wish he'd listened to Mum.

The flight through the night had taken its toll,
They'd left England behind and reached the North Pole.
Billy was battered - bruised black and blue,
Could all that was happening really be true?

Through the mist was a castle with huge silver gates,
Guarded by polar bears gliding on skates.
He was marched through the door, past the blood-thirsty bears,
And told to start climbing the steep flight of stairs.

Five storeys up, a large door opened wide,
And Billy was silently ushered inside.
He found himself stood in a cavernous hall,
With the head of a moose adorning each wall.

A hungry grey wolf stripped meat from a bone,
And a goblin stared down from a gleaming glass throne.
Young Billy was set to find out to his cost,
That this was the home of the evil Jack Frost.

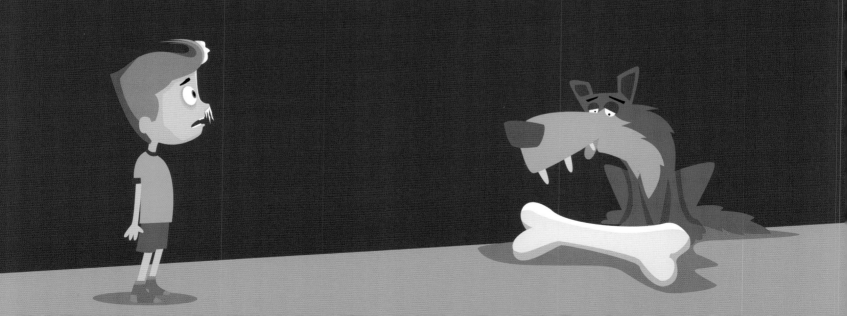

Slippery Jack was the strangest of creatures,
With emerald eyes and razor-sharp features.
He pointed at Billy and the future turned bleak,
As the ice goblin grinned and started to speak.

"So, you like to be cold? Well, I'll give you no choice,"
He shouted at Billy in a thin, squeaky voice.
"For the rest of your days, it will be in my power,
To keep you locked up in the castle's high tower."

SO YOU LIKE TO BE

Billy was forced to climb several miles high,
Up a stone spiral staircase snaking into the sky.
The air was so cold, he could see his breath freeze,
It might even have been minus 50 degrees.

When they finally came to a small wooden door,
The boy was pushed through like a prisoner of war.
Inside it was empty - the tower was bare,
He was lost and alone without even a chair.

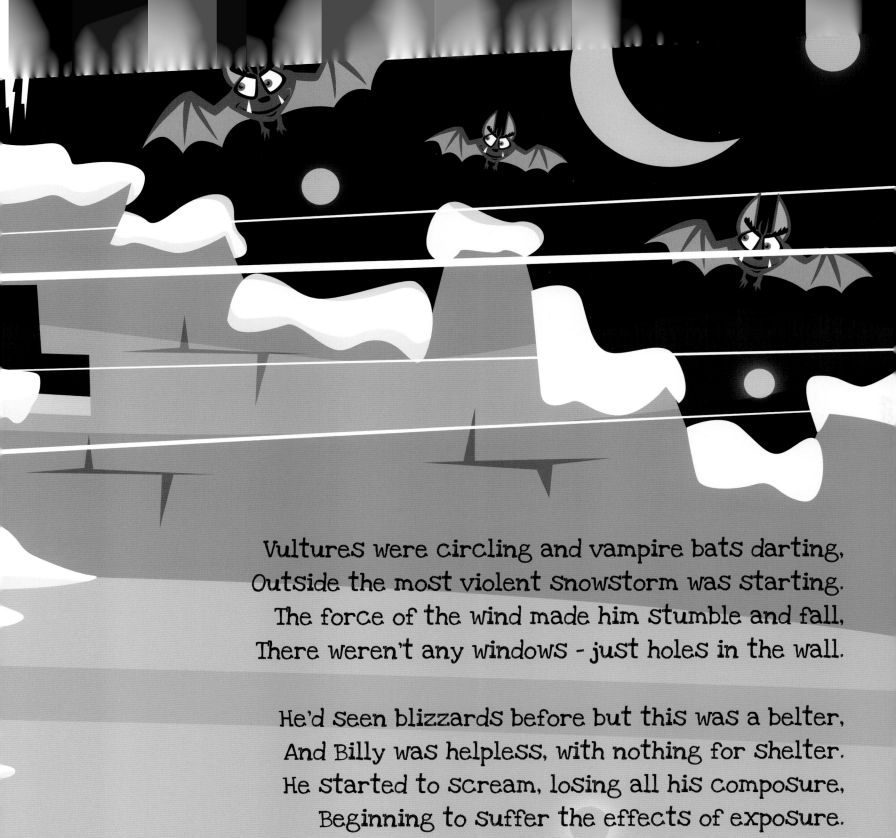

Vultures were circling and vampire bats darting,
Outside the most violent snowstorm was starting.
The force of the wind made him stumble and fall,
There weren't any windows - just holes in the wall.

He'd seen blizzards before but this was a belter,
And Billy was helpless, with nothing for shelter.
He started to scream, losing all his composure,
Beginning to suffer the effects of exposure.

Minutes from death, he curled up in a heap,
Fighting for breath, he slipped into a sleep.
And there on the wind, he heard someone say:
"Billy, wake up, we must be on our way...
You don't need to worry, there's plenty of room,
Up here on the back of my magical broom."
Was it a dream, was he light in the head?
No, he wasn't mistaken, it was old Frozen Fred!

Billy came to his senses with a frightening jolt,
As the tower was struck by a fierce lightning bolt.
He jumped up on the broomstick and WHOOSH - they were off,
But the air was so raw, it made Billy cough.

He held on for dear life and gave Fred a squeeze,
By now he was shaking and starting to sneeze.
Never before had he felt quite so ill,
Like his Mum said, he'd caught a terrible chill.

There were blinding white flashes above and below them,
Zooming in for the kill were six flying snowmen.
They were all throwing snowballs but Billy kept ducking,
Avoiding the missiles the snowmen were chucking.

Fred flew into a dive but the snowmen gave chase,
And a snowball hit Billy slap bang in the face.
Exhausted, defeated, it was all he could take,
Knocked from the broom, he plunged into a lake.

Through a hole in the ice, he dropped like a stone,
In water so cold, he was chilled to the bone.
Too frozen to swim, he just kept sinking down,
Deeper and deeper, he was going to drown.

Floating past penguins and strange kinds of fish,
He closed his eyes tight and made one last wish:
"Please don't leave me here, afraid and alone,
I don't want to die - I just want to go home."

Just then, Frozen Fred, our white knight, our hero,
Cut through the gloom like a great white torpedo.
He scooped up the boy and burst into the sky,
He had Billy back home in the blink of an eye.

When Billy woke up, he was in his own bed,
With all kinds of thoughts spinning round in his head.
He pushed back the covers and quickly got dressed,
This time remembering to put on a vest.

He ran into the garden and gasped as he found,
There by the shed, a small snowy mound.
With the sun coming out, Fred just couldn't stay,
The brave little snowman had melted away.

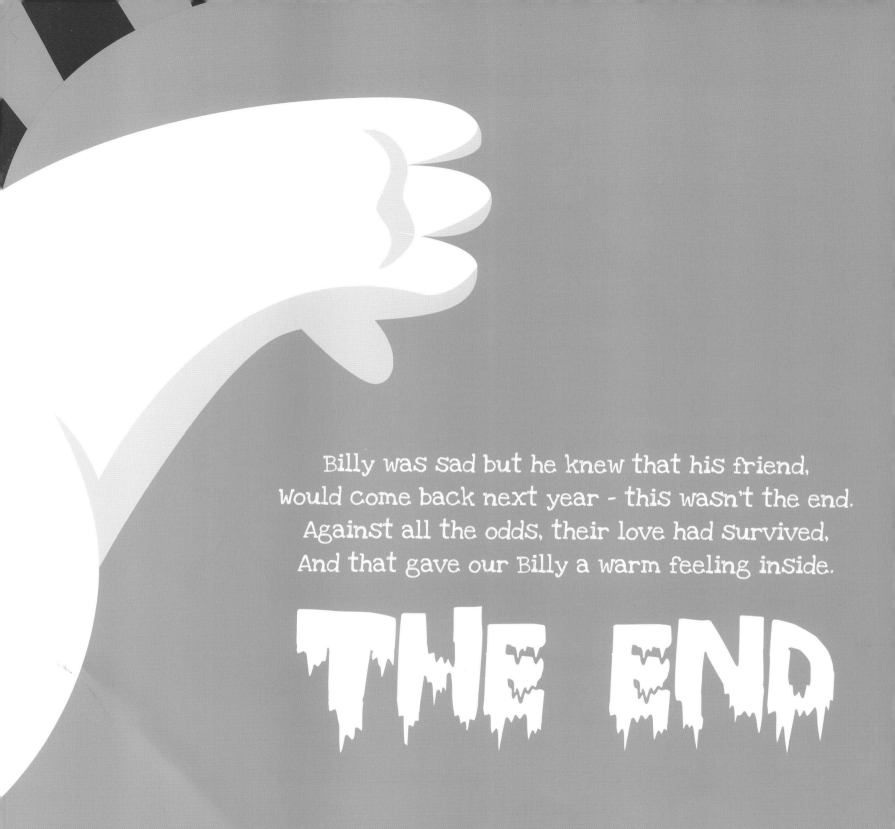

Billy was sad but he knew that his friend,
Would come back next year - this wasn't the end.
Against all the odds, their love had survived,
And that gave our Billy a warm feeling inside.

THE END

And the MONSTROUS moral of this story?

If your Mum tells you to wrap up warm,
don't give her a frosty reception!